CLEMENTINE ROSE

and the
Seaside Escape

Also by Jacqueline Harvey

Clementine Rose and the Surprise Visitor
Clementine Rose and the Pet Day Disaster
Clementine Rose and the Perfect Present
Clementine Rose and the Farm Fiasco
Clementine Rose and the Treasure Box
Clementine Rose and the Famous Friend
Clementine Rose and the Ballet Break-In

Alice-Miranda at School
Alice-Miranda on Holiday
Alice-Miranda Takes the Lead
Alice-Miranda at Sea
Alice-Miranda in New York
Alice-Miranda Shows the Way
Alice-Miranda in Paris
Alice-Miranda Shines Bright
Alice-Miranda in Japan
Alice-Miranda at Camp

CLEMENTINE ROSE

and the
Seaside Escape

Jacqueline Harvey

RED FOX

CLEMENTINE ROSE AND THE SEASIDE ESCAPE
A RED FOX BOOK 978 1 849 41875 1

Published in Great Britain by Red Fox,
an imprint of Random House Children's Publishers UK
A Penguin Random House Company

Penguin
Random House
UK

Originally published in Australia by Random House Australia in 2014

This edition published 2015

1 3 5 7 9 10 8 6 4 2

Text copyright © Jacqueline Harvey, 2014

Penguin Random House is committed to a sustainable future for our
business, our readers and our planet. This book is made from
Forest Stewardship Council ® certified paper.

MIX
Paper from
responsible sources
FSC® C018179

Set in ITC Century

RANDOM HOUSE CHILDREN'S PUBLISHERS UK
61–63 Uxbridge Road, London W5 5SA

www.**randomhousechildrens**.co.uk
www.**totallyrandombooks**.co.uk
www.**randomhouse**.co.uk

Addresses for companies within The Random House Group Limited
can be found at: www.randomhouse.co.uk/offices.htm

THE RANDOM HOUSE GROUP Limited Reg. No. 954009

A CIP catalogue record for this book is available from the British Library.

Printed and bound by CPI Group (UK) Ltd, Croydon, CR0 4YY

*For Ian, who makes me laugh,
and for Nana and Grandad,
and Mum and Dad, who gave me
many great memories of seaside escapes*

A MINOR DELAY

Clementine Rose leaned between the front seats of Uncle Digby's ancient Morris Minor. She looked up at her great-aunt Violet, who had insisted on travelling in the front.

'Is it . . .' Clementine paused. 'Is it an old person?' she asked with a frown.

Aunt Violet turned and curled her lip. 'Who are you calling old? Unless you mean him.' She glanced at Digby Pertwhistle, who was in the driver's seat.

Clementine shook her head. 'No.'

Aunt Violet smiled smugly.

'I meant both of you,' Clementine said.

The grin slid from the woman's lips.

Clementine's mother, Lady Clarissa, was wedged in the back seat with Lavender and Clementine. Before Aunt Violet could erupt, she called out. 'Is it the owl on Uncle Digby's key ring?'

'Yes, it is. Thank goodness that's over,' Aunt Violet harrumphed. 'I've had quite enough of I Spy for one day.'

'But it's Mummy's turn,' said Clementine.

'Godfathers! Can't you just look at the scenery, Clementine?' Aunt Violet protested.

Clementine wrinkled her nose.

The little car puttered to the top of another rise. They had been driving for a couple of hours now. They had passed green fields dotted with oak trees and sheep, lush forests, and now the landscape had opened up again.

'Look!' Clementine shouted, bouncing up and down in her seat.

'Yes, yes, we can all see it,' said Aunt Violet. But even she couldn't suppress the start of a smile.

The ocean spread out before them, twinkling in the afternoon sun. There was a pretty village dotted with whitewashed houses and a perfect crescent beach tucked in between a little harbour and a rocky headland. Further around, the green hills looked as if they rolled all the way to the sandy shore.

'It's beautiful,' Clementine gasped.

'It certainly is,' said Digby. 'And just as I remember it from when I was a boy.'

'I'm surprised you can recall anything that far back,' Aunt Violet teased.

'Don't you worry, Miss Appleby. I have a mind like a steel trap.' Digby tapped his left temple and winked in the old woman's direction.

Aunt Violet rolled her eyes.

'Can we go to the beach this afternoon?' Clementine asked.

'Mmm, I think perhaps we should get settled and then take a walk around the village.

Remember, we've got a whole week, Clemmie,' her mother replied.

'Do you really think those builders will have the new roof on in a week?' Aunt Violet asked. 'They looked an untrustworthy lot, if you ask me.'

'Aunt Violet, I've known Mr Hubbard since I was a little girl and I thought you'd much rather have a holiday by the sea than be woken by builders in the rafters above your bed,' Clarissa replied.

Aunt Violet sighed. 'Yes, yes, you've made your point. In fact, I don't know why we couldn't have stayed for two weeks. One seems a bit stingy, really.'

'One is all I could afford,' Lady Clarissa reminded her aunt.

'I suppose it's for the best. I couldn't bear to leave Pharaoh for longer. I do hope that cat of Mrs Mogg's doesn't lead the dear boy astray,' said Aunt Violet. 'I've heard Claws is a bit of a traveller too.'

Pharaoh was Aunt Violet's sphynx cat.

He was quite possibly the strangest creature Clementine had ever seen, all wrinkly and hairless. But he and Clementine's teacup pig, Lavender, had fallen madly in love, and Clementine adored him too. The only problem was that Pharaoh had a terrible habit of escaping. Aunt Violet had thought about taking him along for the week but, after he'd gone missing for an entire day yet again, she decided it was safer to leave him with the local shopkeeper. Mrs Mogg vowed to keep him under lock and key.

Penberthy House had been in need of a new roof for some time but a recent heavy downpour confirmed that it could wait no longer. Clementine, her mother, Uncle Digby and even Aunt Violet couldn't find enough buckets to collect the drips. As luck would have it, Lady Clarissa had hosted two beautiful weddings in recent months, which had given her enough money to have the roof replaced, as well as a few other minor repairs. The holiday was a lovely bonus.

'What will our hotel be like?' Clementine asked.

'Watertight, I hope,' Aunt Violet smirked.

'Of course it will be,' Clarissa laughed. 'And it's a guesthouse, not a hotel. So I imagine it will be almost like staying with friends. Mrs Dent sounded lovely on the telephone.'

'What's the difference between a guesthouse and a hotel, Mummy?' Clementine asked.

'Not much, darling. It will just be a lot cosier,' Clarissa replied.

Digby Pertwhistle crunched the gears as the little car coughed and sputtered on the narrow road to the village. There was one last hill before they would begin their descent.

Aunt Violet shuddered at the noise. 'I don't see why we couldn't have taken my car.'

Digby wrestled the gears again. 'I think that had something to do with you not getting the registration paid in time.'

Aunt Violet pursed her lips and went strangely quiet.

Suddenly there was a loud bang and the little car slowed down. Digby just managed to steer it off the road and onto the grass verge before it rolled to a halt.

'Uh-oh.' Clementine looked at her mother. 'That didn't sound good.'

'Wonderful,' Aunt Violet grouched. 'I might have guessed something like this would happen.'

Digby opened the door and walked to the front of the car. He lifted the bonnet and thick steam poured from the engine bay.

'You stay here, darling,' said Lady Clarissa before she hopped out to join him.

Aunt Violet wound down the window. 'Hurry up, Pertwhistle. I'm dying of thirst in here!'

Clementine leaned forward again. 'Are you excited?' she asked her great-aunt.

'About what? The prospect of having to walk the last couple of miles to the village or the fact that we'll be staying in a fleapit of a guesthouse that will be altogether too hot and probably smell like boiled cabbages.'

Clementine frowned. 'I meant are you excited about having a holiday by the sea.' She had no idea why her great-aunt thought the house would smell like cabbages. Penberthy House never did.

'I might be, if we ever get there,' the woman replied.

Clementine thought Aunt Violet was a complicated person. The two of them hadn't exactly hit it off when they first met and they'd certainly had their fair share of run-ins. But more recently the woman had seemed to soften a little, although she was still the grumpiest person Clemmie knew.

'Do you want to hear a poem?' Clementine asked.

'No, not particularly,' Aunt Violet replied, craning her neck to see what was going on in front of the car.

'But it's about you,' Clementine said.

'About me?' Aunt Violet eyed the girl suspiciously.

Clementine nodded. 'It's a limerick. Uncle

Digby taught me how to do them. I've just made up one about you in my head.'

'Well, get on with it,' said Aunt Violet.

Clementine frowned in confusion. 'But . . . you said you didn't want to hear it.'

'And now I've changed my mind.'

Clementine began:

'There once was a lady called Vi
Who accidentally swallowed a fly
It tickled and buzzed
And prickled and fuzzed
'Til she coughed it back into the sky.'

Clementine leaned forward to watch her great-aunt's reaction. 'Did you like it?'

Violet Appleby's lips quivered. 'As a matter of fact, Clementine, I thought it was rather . . . clever.' The old woman's mouth stretched into a smile.

'Uncle Digby told me that Vi was short for Violet, because sometimes he calls you that. So I rhymed "Vi" with "fly",' the girl said with a grin.

'Well, I certainly hope I won't be swallowing any flies on this holiday,' said Aunt Violet. 'And Pertwhistle can stop calling me Vi behind my back too – the cheek of him.' She stuck her head out of the window. 'For heaven's sake, what's taking so long?'

A TIGHT SQUEEZE

Just as Aunt Violet was grouching and gasping, a beaten-up tow truck with faded letters on the side pulled off the road ahead of them. A man of sizable proportions slid down from the driver's seat.

He doffed his pork-pie hat towards Lady Clarissa and Uncle Digby. 'Looks like you could do with a hand.'

Lady Clarissa beamed at him. 'Oh, your timing couldn't be better.'

'It's the fan belt,' said Digby, as he held

up the rubbery remains. 'And the old girl's overheated too.'

The man nodded. 'Don't think I have one your size in the truck.'

'We're going to Endersley-on-Sea,' Lady Clarissa explained. 'We could almost walk from here.'

Aunt Violet opened the passenger door and stalked around to the front of the car. 'Well, you could but I'm certainly not!'

The man doffed his hat towards Aunt Violet. 'I can give you a tow, but you'll all have to squash in with me, I'm afraid,' he explained.

Violet Appleby looked at the truck and shuddered. 'I'm not going in that thing.'

'I can send the taxi back for you if you'd prefer.' The man grinned. 'But I know Old Parky's been a bit busy so it might take a while for him to get here. He's the only one in the village.'

Clementine hopped out of the car too.

'Hello there, young lady,' the man said and smiled at her.

'Hello. Are you going to fix our car?' she asked.

'I will when we get it to my workshop. Is anyone else in there?' He already thought there was a surprising number of passengers for such a small vehicle.

'Only Lavender,' Clemmie replied.

Mr Phipps frowned.

'She's my teacup pig. She's not very big at all.' Clementine ran to the back door of the car and retrieved her pet. 'Here she is.'

Lenny tickled the little creature and said, 'Well, it's going to be a tight squeeze, but I'm sure we can all fit in.'

Clementine was almost bursting at the thought of riding in the front of a tow truck.

'Wait until I tell Angus that we got to go in a proper truck,' she said, dancing about.

'If we'd driven a proper car, we wouldn't be going anywhere near that thing you're calling a truck,' Aunt Violet muttered.

Lady Clarissa ignored her. 'Thank you very much, Mr . . .?' She hesitated, waiting for the man to introduce himself.

'The name's Lenny, Lenny Phipps.'

Within a couple of minutes, the little Morris Minor was hooked up to the back of the truck and the family was jammed in along the bench seat. Clementine sat on her mother's lap nursing Lavender, with Aunt Violet beside her next to Mr Phipps. Uncle Digby was squeezed in by the passenger door. With some fiddling about, everyone was strapped in, and soon they were on their way.

WELCOME

It wasn't long before Mr Phipps pulled up outside a pretty whitewashed townhouse in the middle of the village. It was right opposite the harbour, three storeys high with wide bay windows. Out the front was a small garden with neatly clipped hedges and a colourful bed of petunias.

'Is that where we're staying?' Clementine asked. She tried to sound out the name on the front gate. 'En-der-sley-on-Sea Guesthouse.'

Clarissa nodded. 'This is it.'

Digby studied the building. 'I have a feeling I might have stayed here when I was a boy.'

'I hope they've updated things since then,' said Aunt Violet, 'or we might as well have stayed at home and dodged the builders.'

Lenny Phipps and Digby Pertwhistle opened the truck's doors. Aunt Violet and Lady Clarissa breathed out. Clementine gave a big sigh and Lavender grunted loudly.

'I'll help you with your things,' Mr Phipps offered as he hopped out and walked around to Digby's little car.

Digby poked his head back inside the cabin. 'Clarissa, dear, why don't you take everyone inside and I'll sort the rest.'

Lady Clarissa nodded.

'I hope they make a decent cup of tea,' Aunt Violet grumbled. 'I'm parched.'

Clementine picked up Lavender and held her tight. The tiny pig was wearing her sparkly red collar and lead.

'I love this place already,' said Clementine.

Her mother looked at her. 'Already?'

'Yes, because I don't think there are many guesthouses where you can bring pigs.'

Clementine was right about that. Lady Clarissa had called more than a dozen guesthouses and hotels along the coast before she had found this one. The owner, Mrs Dent, said she was happy to have four-legged guests as long as they behaved themselves and were house-trained. Clarissa had mentioned that Lavender was a teacup pig, expecting the woman to change her mind. But Mrs Dent had been delighted by the idea.

The ladies and Clementine made their way through the front gate as Lenny Phipps waved goodbye to them.

Clementine followed her mother into the front hall. There was a small reception desk with a bell, which Clarissa let Clementine ring.

A voice tinkled from down the hallway. 'Hello, hello?'

A woman appeared. She was short and round, with a tummy that looked as soft as a pillow. She reminded Clementine of Mrs Mogg.

'Hello,' said Lady Clarissa. 'You must be Mrs Dent.'

'I am indeed, dear. Rosamund Dent at your service. And you must be Clarissa Appleby.'

Clementine liked Mrs Dent's rosy cheeks and the way her eyes sparkled when she spoke.

'Oh my goodness, is that little Lavender?' She rushed towards Clementine, who was nursing the animal, and leaned down to nuzzle her face against the tiny pig.

Lavender grunted and snuggled Mrs Dent back.

'Oh, she's precious.' Mrs Dent rubbed Lavender's head.

Clementine smiled. 'She likes you.'

'This is my daughter, Clementine, and my aunt, Violet Appleby,' Lady Clarissa explained.

'Good afternoon,' said Aunt Violet.

'Hello,' said Clementine. 'Uncle Digby is outside with Mr Phipps. Our car broke down so we had to get it towed.'

'Oh, dear me, what a dreadful way to start a holiday,' said the old woman.

'Yes, you can't imagine –' Aunt Violet began to grizzle. She was all set to continue when Mrs Dent stopped her in her tracks.

'How about I show you to your rooms and then I'll pop the kettle on. And I hope you like strawberry sponge cake.'

'Yes, please!' Clementine clapped her hands together.

'Do you have a full house at the moment?' Lady Clarissa asked as the woman walked around the reception desk.

'No, dear, there's just your group, and my grandchildren, who are visiting. Their parents have gone away for a couple of weeks, so they're all mine. You picked a good time to come – things will get much busier towards the end of the month.'

Clementine's eyes lit up. 'How old are your grandchildren?'

'Freddy is almost eight and his sister Della is ten,' Mrs Dent replied. 'And I'm sure they will love having an extra playmate for the holidays. I'm a bit boring, you see. I'm good with making cakes and reading stories but when it comes to the beach, I'm not much fun at all.'

'Like Aunt Violet,' Clementine replied. 'She's good at stories too, but I don't think she'll take me swimming.'

Violet peered down at the child. 'Says who?'

'Well, you said that you don't like sand, and the beach is covered in it,' Clementine explained.

Aunt Violet raised her eyebrows. 'We'll see about that.'

Mrs Dent picked up three keys on large wooden key rings and handed them to Lady Clarissa. 'Mr Pertwhistle and Miss Appleby have their own rooms and there's another for you and Clementine.'

'Perfect,' said Lady Clarissa.

'I've put you all together on the first floor.'

Clementine looked around her. The house was freshly painted, with pretty blue wallpaper and lots of white furniture, but she didn't think it was as lovely as her own home – even with the drips and peeling paint. There were no portraits, either. Clementine thought about the pictures of her long-departed grandparents on the walls in the grand entry at Penberthy House. She hoped they wouldn't be too lonely without her chatting to them and practising her poems.

'Come along, then. I'll take you upstairs,' said Mrs Dent.

'Where are your grandchildren?' Clementine asked as they trooped down the hall.

'They'll be back soon. I sent them to the shop to pick up some more vegetables for dinner.'

Lavender grunted loudly at this.

'Yes, I'm sure you like vegetables too, little one,' Mrs Dent said with a laugh.

Clementine giggled.

A POEM

In no time flat, Uncle Digby had delivered the suitcases to the rooms and everyone had unpacked, ready to start their holiday. Mr Phipps towed Uncle Digby's car to his workshop. It wasn't a bother, as they weren't planning to use the car at all. They wouldn't need to, because the guesthouse was right in the middle of the village, with the beach just across the road.

Downstairs, the sweet smell of freshly baked cakes filled the air and the long dining room table was perfectly laid with fine china and pretty floral napkins.

'Mrs Dent, you really didn't have to go to all this trouble,' Clarissa protested when she saw the room. 'We'd have been just as happy in the kitchen.'

'Oh, my dear, I couldn't do that to you on your first afternoon. But I might from now on, if you really don't mind. I've got a beautiful old table in there – perhaps we can have breakfast and lunch in the kitchen and I'll use the dining room in the evenings,' the old woman suggested.

Clementine thought Mrs Dent had the loveliest smile wrinkles she'd ever seen.

'Well, I know that Clementine and Uncle Digby and I would be very happy with that, and Aunt Violet will just have to get used to it,' said Lady Clarissa firmly.

Aunt Violet appeared in the doorway. 'What will I have to get used to?' She'd changed out of the navy pants-suit she'd worn for travelling and was now in a smart pair of cream trousers with a red silk blouse and matching ballet flats. Clementine thought that she looked very stylish, although perhaps a bit overdressed for a beach holiday.

'I was just saying that Mrs Dent didn't have to go to all this trouble for us. We'd be happy taking tea in the kitchen,' Clarissa said.

'Oh yes, absolutely,' Aunt Violet agreed.

Clarissa was surprised to hear it. So was Clementine, who asked if her great-aunt was feeling all right.

'Yes, of course. A bit thirsty, but I'm fine,' the old woman replied. 'Why do you ask?'

'Well, at home you're always grouching that the guests get to use the dining room and we have to stay in the kitchen,' Clementine explained.

'Just as long as I don't have to do any work for the next week, I don't mind where Mrs Dent feeds us,' Aunt Violet said.

Clementine stared at her, puzzled. 'But you don't do any work at home.'

'I beg your pardon, young lady,' the old woman snapped. 'I'll have you know I'm a very busy person.'

'Usually busy complaining,' said Uncle Digby under his breath.

Aunt Violet spun around and narrowed her eyes. 'I heard that, Pertwhistle.'

'Why don't you all come and have a drink and something to eat?' said Mrs Dent. She winked at Clementine. She could see that her guests were going to keep her entertained.

Digby Pertwhistle helped seat the ladies, as he was used to doing at home. He glanced up at Mrs Dent, and his forehead creased. 'I can't help thinking I've met you before, Mrs Dent.'

She looked up. 'You know, I've been thinking the same thing. You look familiar but I don't recognise your name.'

'Has the house always taken guests?' Digby asked.

The woman shook her head. 'No, my late husband and I bought it as a family home – from my aunt and uncle, actually. They used to come here for holidays. When Hector passed away a few years ago, I turned it into a guesthouse. I couldn't stand rattling around here on my own.'

Digby frowned. There was a memory scratching inside his head.

'So much for that mind like a steel trap, eh, Pertwhistle?' Aunt Violet teased. 'More like a sieve, don't you think?'

Digby grinned. 'Well, as Clementine pointed out earlier, neither of us are spring chickens any more.'

Just as Mrs Dent finished pouring the tea and Lady Clarissa served the cake, the front door banged and there was the sound of feet running down the hallway.

'I think the children are back,' said Mrs Dent. She went to intercept them.

'What have you done with Lavender?' Uncle Digby asked.

'She's having a sleep in her basket,' Clementine said. 'She was 'sausted.'

Clementine took a bite of her sponge cake and picked up the glass of lemonade Mrs Dent had poured for her.

'This is almost as good as Uncle Pierre's cake,' said Clemmie, while munching happily.

Mrs Dent appeared in the doorway with two children. 'I'd like you to meet my grand-daughter, Della, and my grandson, Freddy.'

The girl was tall and thin with light-brown hair pulled into a ponytail. She had piercing green eyes and wore green shorts and a pink t-shirt with a glittery heart in the centre. The boy was blond-haired and blue-eyed and, on first glance, looked more like Clementine than his sister.

There was a chorus of hellos from the adults.

'You said she was older,' Della whispered to her grandmother. 'She's just a baby.'

'Della,' Mrs Dent chided.

Clementine looked at the girl. She wore nice clothes but her face seemed the complete opposite of her grandmother's. There was no sparkling and twinkling. Della looked as if she had swallowed something nasty.

'Freddy, Della, aren't you going to say hello to Clementine?' Mrs Dent asked.

'Hello.' Freddy gave a shy smile.

'Hello,' Della said with a pout.

Clementine's tummy twinged. Her mother looked at her and nodded.

'Hello,' Clementine replied.

Mrs Dent set about cutting some more cake for the children and directed them to sit at the other end of the table, near Clementine.

Soon the adults were chatting about this and that and the children were left to their own devices.

'How old are you?' Della asked Clementine with a mouthful of cake.

'I'm five and a half,' the younger girl replied.

Della sighed. 'Granny said that I'd have someone to play with but you're way too young. I only play with people who are seven and over.'

'I can do lots of things a seven-year-old can,' Clementine said hopefully.

'Like what?' Della challenged her.

'I can skip with a rope,' Clementine said.

'Any baby can do that,' Della scoffed.

'I can read lots of hard words and I can make up poems,' Clementine said.

'No, you can't.' Della shook her head. 'Five-year-olds are too stupid to make up poems.'

'That's not true,' Clementine said. She wondered why this girl was so mean and bossy. It seemed strange that her grandmother was about the kindest person Clemmie had met, but Della was crabbier than her teacher, Mrs Bottomley, and Joshua Tribble put together.

'I can make up a poem about you,' Clementine blurted.

Della's eyes narrowed. 'No, you can't.'

'Yes, I can,' Clementine nodded.

'Show me then,' said Della.

Clementine was trying to remember what Uncle Digby had taught her about limericks.

'There once was a girl called Della . . .' Clementine stopped. She was thinking about the next line. It was hard to come up with something that rhymed with that name.

Uncle Digby had half an ear on what was happening and leaned over and whispered something to Clementine.

The child smiled.

'Well, get on with it,' Della said.

Clementine tried again: 'There once was a girl called Della, who was in love with a cute little fella –'

Della glared at Clementine. 'I don't love anybody!'

'But I haven't finished yet.' Clementine felt her bottom lip wobble. She hadn't meant to upset the girl.

'Come on, Freddy. We're going upstairs.' Della pushed back her chair and pinched her brother's arm.

'Ow,' the boy complained.

'Della, why don't you take Clementine with you too?' Mrs Dent suggested.

But the girl raced off. Freddy turned and looked at Clementine. He gave an embarrassed half-smile and scurried from the room.

A fat tear sprouted in the corner of Clementine's eye.

'Are you all right, darling?' her mother asked.

Clementine brushed it away and nodded.

Digby Pertwhistle leaned over and kissed the top of the child's head. 'Don't worry about her, Clemmie. I don't think she appreciates poetry.'

'Did Della say something to upset you?' Mrs Dent asked from her seat at the other end of the table.

'She'd better not have,' Aunt Violet said tersely.

Clementine shook her head. She didn't want to get anyone in trouble, especially not if she had to share the house with them for the next week.

FREDDY

'Shall we go for a walk around the village?' Lady Clarissa asked Clementine as they climbed the stairs to their room.

Clementine nodded. 'Will Aunt Violet and Uncle Digby come too?'

Her mother shook her head. 'Uncle Digby's going to have a lie down and I suspect Aunt Violet might be planning a rest too.'

'Is Uncle Digby all right?' Clemmie's voice was anxious. Since he'd spent time in hospital earlier in the year, she worried a lot about the old man.

'Oh, yes, darling. I think the drive just took it out of him – and having the car break down was a little bit stressful.'

'Especially with Aunt Violet there,' said Clementine.

'Yes, *especially* with Aunt Violet there,' her mother agreed.

The pair walked along the hall to their room at the front of the hotel. It had a beautiful view over the harbour. Aunt Violet's room was even bigger, with a bay window seat. Uncle Digby's room was on the other side of the hall, looking over the back garden.

Lavender appeared to be snoozing in her basket. But as soon as Clementine picked up the sparkly red lead that was hanging on the wardrobe door, the tiny pig scrambled to her feet and danced about at the child's knees.

'Someone's keen to go exploring,' said Lady Clarissa as she grabbed a pink cardigan for Clementine and threw a white jacket around her own shoulders.

Clementine snapped Lavender's lead onto her collar and the trio set off.

Downstairs, they bumped into Mrs Dent, who was balancing a stack of plates from the dining room.

'Have a good walk,' the old woman said with a smile. She carried on into the kitchen.

'Oh, I forgot the camera,' Lady Clarissa said. 'I'll just dash up and get it.'

Clementine was left standing on her own in the entrance hall. 'Mrs Dent's lovely, isn't she, Lavender?' Clementine said to the little pig. 'But I'm not sure about Della. I don't think she likes me.'

The floorboards creaked and Clementine spun around. She saw a face peeking out from one of the doorways. It was Freddy.

The boy's blue eyes widened underneath his mop of blond hair. 'Is that a pig?'

Clementine nodded. 'Her name's Lavender.'

'She's cute,' the boy replied as he took some tentative steps towards them. He knelt down and gave Lavender a rub on the neck.

The little pig repaid him by nibbling his fingers.

'That tickles,' he giggled. 'Is she a piglet?'

'No,' Clementine replied. 'She's a teacup pig.'

'Cool!' said the boy. 'I've never seen one before.'

'Where's your sister?' Clementine asked.

'She's making up a dance,' said Freddy. 'She does that all the time.'

'I love dancing,' Clementine said.

Lady Clarissa walked towards the children. 'Hello, Freddy.'

The lad looked up and smiled. 'Hello. Are you going for a walk?'

Clementine nodded.

'Can I come?'

Clarissa looked at her daughter and raised her eyebrows ever so slightly. Clementine smiled and nodded.

'Yes, of course, but you'll have to ask your grandmother,' Clarissa said.

The boy dashed to the kitchen. He was back in no time, grinning. 'Granny said I could go.'

'What about your sister?' Clarissa asked. 'Do you think she'd like to come as well?'

Freddy shook his head firmly. 'No. She's busy.'

'You can be our tour guide,' Clementine said.

Freddy nodded. 'Can we go now?'

Lady Clarissa thought the lad was awfully eager to get moving. He rushed down the hall and wrenched open the front door.

'Come on, there's a lot to see,' the boy said as he held the door open for Lady Clarissa, Clementine and Lavender.

As Freddy pulled it shut behind him, a shrill voice screeched, 'Freddy, where are you? You're supposed to be helping me with my dance.'

There was the sound of a door slamming and pounding feet on the stairs.

Clementine looked back at the house. 'I think that was your sister.'

'I didn't hear anything,' the boy replied and bounded off down the garden path.

Clementine looked at her mother, who shrugged, and the pair kept walking.

ENDERSLEY~ ON~SEA

reddy turned out to be a wonderful guide indeed. He introduced Clementine and her mother to Mrs Lee, who owned the village store, and Mr Alessi, the fish and chip shop owner. Mr Alessi's brothers ran a small fleet of fishing boats that were moored in the harbour. Freddy took them past Mr Phipps's workshop, where Uncle Digby's little car was hoisted up high. Lastly, they met Mrs Pink, who owned the bakery and tearooms.

Clementine thought the village was one of

the prettiest she'd ever seen. She loved the whitewashed houses and shops and grand sandstone buildings. Just past the harbour was the beach. On a grassy knoll behind that was a caravan park with mobile homes of all shapes and sizes dotted across green lawns. There were tents too. Some were small, while others looked almost like houses.

'Granny says the caravan park has the best spot in town,' Freddy explained as they walked along the seawall that separated the harbour and the beach.

'Can we stay in a caravan one day, Mummy?' Clementine asked. She liked the thought of a little home where everything was in reach. It would be different to Penberthy House, which was enormous.

'That's a lovely idea, sweetheart,' Lady Clarissa said with a smile. 'Perhaps we can save that for a holiday for the two of us. I don't think Aunt Violet would approve.'

Clementine giggled at the thought of her great-aunt sleeping in a caravan, or even worse, a tent. 'Can we walk on the sand?'

Lady Clarissa nodded. 'Yes, of course. Give me your shoes and you and Freddy can take Lavender for a run along the water's edge.'

Clementine kicked off her sandals and Freddy did too. She carried Lavender down a set of old concrete steps and then set the pig down on the beach. Clementine and Freddy laughed as Lavender hopped about, unaccustomed to the strange texture under her trotters. Clarissa snapped some photographs of the unsuspecting children.

'She's a rabbit pig,' Freddy said as Lavender leapt into the air, her curly tail wriggling madly.

Clementine unclipped her lead and began to run towards the sea. The water was almost flat, with just the tiniest of waves curling onto the shore. The little pig chased after her but stopped when she reached the wet sand.

Lavender put one foot forward, dipping her trotter into a puddle, then she squealed and raced away towards Freddy.

Clarissa laughed and sat down on the steps, enjoying the warm sun on her back.

Eventually Clementine coaxed Lavender into the shallows. She and Freddy hooted with laughter as they ran in and out with Lavender chasing them.

After a while, Clementine took Lavender up onto the dry sand and the two of them plonked down. Freddy sat beside them

'What class are you in?' Clementine asked the boy.

'Year two,' Freddy replied.

'I'm in kindy,' Clementine said. 'I love school.'

'School's okay.' Freddy shrugged. 'But I like holidays better.'

Clementine stroked Lavender's tummy and the little pig grunted.

'Where are your mum and dad?' she asked, looking up at the sandy-haired boy.

'Dad had a conference and Mum went too, so that's why we're staying with Granny. Where's your dad?' Freddy asked.

Clementine paused. She remembered when she told Angus Archibald that her father was a mystery and he'd told her that was stupid.

'I don't know,' she replied. 'I've never met him.'

'You have a nice mum,' Freddy said, smiling. 'And your Uncle Digby is funny . . . but I'm not sure about that old lady.'

Clementine giggled. 'You mean Aunt Violet? She looks scarier than she is.'

'Do you want me to show you the rock pools?' Freddy asked.

Clementine nodded. Lavender was lying down with her eyes almost closed. Lady Clarissa wandered down onto the beach.

'Mummy, can we go to the rock pools, please?' Clementine asked.

'Yes, of course. I'll come too. Make sure you put your sandals on first. Those rocks can be sharp,' Lady Clarissa replied.

The children put their shoes back on, and raced towards the far end of the beach. A sheer cliff rose up from the rocks. With the harbour wall at one end and the cliff at the other, the beach was a perfect crescent. Lady Clarissa and Lavender followed behind. Lavender was busy investigating the sand, snout down.

'Look at this,' Freddy called as he jumped across a puddle onto the start of the rocky outcrop. He crouched down and stared into the clear pool.

'What is it?' Clementine squatted down beside him.

'Hang on.' Freddy scampered away then returned with a thin piece of driftwood. He poked it into the water.

A tentacle reached out and wrapped around the stick.

'It's an octopus!' Clementine gasped. She'd never seen one in real life.

'Isn't it cool?' Freddy said as the creature played tug of war with him. After a few seconds, the octopus released the stick and hid beneath a rock in the pool.

'What else is there?' Clementine asked eagerly.

Freddy leapt over another puddle towards a much bigger pool.

'Look at this!' he shouted as Clementine picked her way carefully over to join him.

A tiny crab scurried sideways, then was joined by several more. Clementine stared into the water, watching a large crab that was moving slowly along the bottom of the pool.

After a minute, she glanced up and noticed the way the rock shelf jutted out towards the sea. 'What's on the other side?' Clementine asked.

'There's another beach and something really amazing,' said Freddy.

'Mummy, can we go around further?' Clementine called to Lady Clarissa, who was now sitting on a large rock with Lavender beside her.

Lady Clarissa's voice carried back to them on the wind. 'Yes, darling, just be careful.'

Freddy led the way.

'This is a proper adventure,' said Clementine with a smile.

The children jumped and hopped their way across the uneven surface, careful not to slip into the pools. Around the point, the rock shelf curved back towards the cliffs. A few steps below them was a narrow inlet, and on the other side another tiny beach, with a patch of green grass behind it.

'Can you see anything?' Freddy asked, as he pointed at the cliff face on the other side of the inlet.

Clementine looked at the vines that tumbled over the top of the ledge and hung down like a veil.

'What is it?' she said, squinting.

Freddy pointed again. 'Just there.'

Clementine gasped. Hidden behind the vines was the outline of an opening. 'It's a cave!'

Freddy grinned.

'Have you been in there?' Clementine asked.

'Yes,' the boy nodded.

'But it's dark and we haven't got a torch,' Clementine said.

'I've got a special torch,' Freddy said, 'but it's at home.'

The boy made his way down the rocks, then jumped across the shallow inlet to the cave opening. He pulled the vines to one side. Clementine stayed back.

'We could bring your torch and look in there tomorrow,' Clementine suggested.

Freddy grinned at her. 'That's the best idea. It's not that scary but it will be better with a torch.'

He was trying to sound brave. When Freddy and Della had discovered the cave on their last visit to Endersley-on-Sea, Della had called him a sook because he hadn't wanted to go in. She'd pushed him through the vines and the darkness had covered him like a blanket. But he was sure it would be okay with a torch.

'We'll come back tomorrow,' said Freddy. He turned and jumped back across the narrow inlet and over the rocks to Clementine. The two children scurried back towards the main beach. They'd just rounded the headland when a voice screeched above the sound of the waves.

'Freddy! You have to come home. NOW!'

Freddy and Clementine reached Clarissa, who was looking towards the village end of the beach and the source of the noise.

The boy caught his breath and Clementine noticed he was jiggling nervously, as if he needed to go to the toilet. Della was standing at the top of the stairs with her hands on her hips. Her hair was blowing in the breeze and she looked a bit like a lion – only twice as fierce.

'It sounds like someone is looking for you Freddy,' said Lady Clarissa. She squinted at Della in the distance.

'She can wait,' Freddy said, his voice wavering.

Clarissa was not so sure about that. She turned her attention back to Freddy and Clementine.

'Did you find anything interesting?' she asked.

Clementine and Freddy nodded.

'We saw an octopus,' Clementine said excitedly. 'And a cave. Didn't we, Freddy?'

The shouting was getting louder. Freddy looked past Lady Clarissa at his sister, who was now running along the beach towards them. He said nothing.

'Are you all right?' Clementine asked.

'I-I have to go,' Freddy said, and raced away towards Della.

'Thanks for the tour,' Clementine called after him. She watched as he reached his sister halfway along the beach. Clementine could just make out snatches of Della's words. She sounded angry. She grabbed the boy's shoulder and marched him away.

'I think Freddy's in trouble,' said Clementine. As she watched, Della pushed him hard in the middle of his back.

'Oh dear,' Lady Clarissa said. 'We'll have to make sure we ask Della to come tomorrow too.'

Clementine frowned. Freddy was lovely, but Della was something altogether different.

TIED UP

When Clementine and her mother returned to the house, Uncle Digby and Aunt Violet were in the front sitting room.

Uncle Digby looked up from the newspaper on his lap. 'Did you have a good walk?'

'We saw an octopus and some crabs and a cave!' Clementine enthused. 'But then Della came to get Freddy. So Mummy and I went for a walk around the harbour and I had an ice-cream and Lavender licked up the drips.'

'Look at that pig!' Aunt Violet shook her head at Lavender, who was encrusted with sand. 'You'll have to give her a rinse, Clementine.'

Rosamund Dent appeared in the doorway behind Clarissa. 'Oh, a bit of sand never hurt anyone,' she said with a smile. 'When you live by the sea you come to expect it. Now, would anyone like anything before I get started on dinner?'

Digby shook his head. 'No, thank you, Mrs Dent.'

'I wouldn't mind another cup of tea,' said Aunt Violet.

'You might turn into a cup of tea, the amount you drink,' Digby said pointedly.

'Well, you could get it for me,' Aunt Violet snapped, 'and save Mrs Dent the trouble.'

'Oh, it's no trouble. You're on holidays,' Mrs Dent smiled.

Digby hoisted himself to his feet. 'I'll come and give you a hand.'

Aunt Violet studied Mrs Dent and wondered how the woman's face could look like a sunbeam even when she wasn't smiling.

'I think we'll give Lavender a quick rinse in the shower. Clementine, you might like to have a bath too. Then you can be ready for bed straight after supper,' Clarissa suggested.

'But Mummy, we're on holidays,' Clementine said. 'Can I stay up later?'

'Of course, darling. I just thought you might like to feel a bit less salty,' her mother said.

'Dinner will be ready in about an hour,' said Mrs Dent, 'so you've got plenty of time. If you don't mind helping with the tea, Mr Pertwhistle, I might try to get those two of mine through the bath as well.'

'Certainly. And please call me Digby.'

'In that case, you must call me Rosamund,' Mrs Dent replied.

'And you can call me nauseated,' Violet Appleby muttered.

'I'm sorry Miss Appleby, did you say something?' Mrs Dent asked.

The old woman pursed her lips. 'No, I'm just a little parched.'

Clarissa stared at her aunt. She'd heard her perfectly.

Clementine scooped Lavender into her arms and followed her mother upstairs. There was no sign of Freddy or his sister anywhere. She wondered if their bedrooms were at the back of the house or above them, on the second floor. Wherever they were, they were awfully quiet.

Clementine took her bath while her mother gave Lavender a quick rinse in the shower. The little pig enjoyed the warm water, snapping at the spray and dancing about on the tiles. Clementine got dressed and wrapped Lavender in a towel.

'You smell nice,' Clementine said and nuzzled the pig's face. Lavender repaid her with a nibble on the nose.

'Clemmie, I'm going to get changed for dinner,' said her mother. 'Why don't you see if Freddy and Della want to play?'

Clementine took Lavender and headed down the hall. She didn't notice Della sitting near the top of the stairs leading up to the second floor.

'Why do you have a pig?' the child asked tartly.

Clementine spun around. 'Oh hello,' she said.

'Well?' Della stood up and stumped down the stairs towards Clementine. 'Why don't you have a normal pet like a dog or a cat or a guinea pig?'

'Mummy won her at the fair,' Clementine replied. Lavender looked up at her mistress and gave a squeak. 'Aunt Violet has a cat. His name is Pharaoh and he's a sphynx.'

'No, he's not. The Sphinx is a half-lion, half-man statue in Egypt. It's not a cat,' Della said.

'Yes, he is. He's bald and wrinkly and sometimes he scares the guests at home,' Clementine replied. 'I didn't know what he was at first because he doesn't look like any other cats I know.'

'Well, I have a pet python,' the girl said, her eyes narrowing. 'It's five metres long and we feed it all sorts of meaty little creatures.'

Clementine gulped. 'What's its name?'

Della hesitated for a moment. 'It's . . . it's Polly, if you must know.'

'That's a good name for a python,' Clemmie said quietly.

'Aren't you scared?' Della demanded.

Clementine drew herself up tall and shook her head. 'No, I'm sure that your granny doesn't let her roam around the house. I have a toy python. Once, I left it in the Rose Room and the lady who was staying there screamed and screamed because she thought it was real. It wasn't very good for business because Mummy had to give her a big discount and make her lots of tea so she would calm down.'

Della looked confused.

'We live in a hotel,' added Clementine.

'No, you don't,' the girl said.

Clementine nodded. 'Yes, we do. It's called Penberthy House and it's very big and old and it's getting a new roof, so that's why we've come on holidays.'

'Well, it's not as big as our hotel,' Della snapped.

Clementine looked around her. Penberthy House was much larger and grander than Mrs Dent's guesthouse.

Della glared at her.

'I'm going downstairs now,' Clementine said.

'Why?' Della snapped.

'Because Mummy said I should find Freddy so we can play a game,' Clementine said.

'Do you always do what your mother tells you?' Della asked.

Clementine thought about it and then nodded. 'I try to.'

'You're such a baby. Only babies do everything their mothers tell them,' Della sneered. 'Anyway, Freddy's tied up at the moment.'

Clementine frowned. 'Oh.'

'You can play a game with me instead,' Della said.

Clementine looked at the girl. 'But I thought you only played with people who were over seven.'

'Usually I do. But seeing that there's no one over seven here to play with now, I suppose you'll have to do.'

'You don't have to,' Clementine said.

'Don't you *want* to play with me now?' Della sighed.

'Okay,' Clementine nodded. 'What should we play?'

'Hide-and-seek,' Della said. 'You hide and I'll find you and the pig.'

Clementine smiled. She liked hide-and-seek – especially at home where there were lots of places to disappear. But she had no idea where to hide here. She'd only been downstairs and in her own room with her mother.

'I don't know where to go,' Clementine said.

'Up there.' Della pointed to the top floor. 'But you have to stay on the left-hand side of the stairs.'

Clementine gulped.

'You do know your left and right, don't you?' asked Della.

Clementine nodded. Secretly, she was trying to remember which was which.

'Can Freddy play too?' Clementine asked.

'No. He went to the beach without me, so now I'm playing a game without him,' Della said, flicking her fingernails. 'Well, off you go. I'll count to fifty and then I'm coming to get you.'

Clementine picked up Lavender and scampered up the stairs to the top floor. She reached the landing and looked each way. She couldn't remember if left was this way or that way. There were several doors along both sides of the corridor. Clementine ran to the one furthest along. She pushed it open.

Inside was a pretty room with blue floral wallpaper. There was a large bookshelf and an iron bedstead. Clementine wondered if this was where Della slept. There was another door on the far wall. Clementine turned the handle and found herself in a bathroom. She hid behind the towel hanging on the rail, pulling it down so it skimmed the floor.

Clementine heard a voice in the hallway.

'Ready or not, here I come,' Della shouted. But the footsteps seemed to be running away.

Clementine thought about left and right. Mrs Bottomley had taught the class that the left hand makes the shape of a capital L. Clementine put Lavender down and held up her hands. Oops – she'd turned right at the top of the stairs.

'Come on, Lavender, let's go before we get in trouble.' Clementine picked up the little pig and they dashed out of the bathroom and back through the bedroom. She opened the door and peeked out. Della was nowhere to be seen. Clementine scurried along the hall back to the landing and crouched down beside a fire extinguisher, with Lavender sitting next to her.

'Where are you?' Della called in a singsong voice.

Clementine held her breath. She could feel her heart beating in her ears. The door furthest down the corridor to the left banged and Della stomped outside. Clementine was sure that the girl would spot her but instead she dived through the next door.

'I'm going to find you,' Della cried.

Clementine became aware of a tapping noise.

'What's that?' she whispered and looked at Lavender with a frown. The noise was getting louder. There was a mumbly voice as well as the tapping now.

Della reappeared in the hallway, banging the door shut behind her.

'You'd better not be down the other end or you'll be in trouble, Clementine! I told you not to go there!' Della was stomping towards the child and her pig.

Clementine crouched down as far as she could go and Della walked right past her. Lavender let out a little grunt and the child spun around.

'There you are!' Della pointed her finger. 'How come I didn't see you before?'

Clementine shrugged. 'I'm good at hiding. What's that tapping noise?'

Della listened. 'It's Polly. She wants her dinner.'

Clementine's eyes grew wide. 'I have to go downstairs. I think Mummy's calling me.' She picked up Lavender and scurried away.

'But it's my turn to hide,' Della protested. She pouted and stamped her foot.

Clementine raced down two flights of stairs and along the hall to the kitchen. She pushed her way inside and let out a deep breath.

'Are you all right, dear?' Mrs Dent turned from where she was stirring a huge pot on a gigantic old stove.

Clementine nodded.

Digby Pertwhistle was busy doing a crossword, Lady Clarissa was flicking through one of Mrs Dent's cookbooks and Aunt Violet was sitting at the other end of the table, nibbling a biscuit and drinking tea.

'Would you like a glass of milk and a brownie?' Mrs Dent asked.

Uncle Digby looked up and grinned. 'They're delicious, Clementine.'

'Do you think that's wise, Clemmie? Dinner's almost ready,' her mother asked.

'I'm really hungry.' Clementine climbed onto the chair beside Uncle Digby. Lavender snuffled about the kitchen floor looking for crumbs. 'And I promise to eat all my dinner.'

Clarissa smiled. 'All right. We are on holidays, after all. An extra treat won't hurt.'

'What have you been up to?' Uncle Digby asked.

'I was playing hide-and-seek with Della,' Clementine said.

Her mother smiled. 'Oh, that's good, darling.'

Clementine turned to Mrs Dent. 'Does Polly live upstairs?'

'Polly?' Mrs Dent frowned as she poured Clementine's milk.

'Della said that she has a python called Polly,' Clementine explained.

'Della has a good imagination, that's what she has.' Mrs Dent rolled her eyes, wondering what sort of dreadful tales her granddaughter had been filling Clementine's head with.

'I heard something banging and Della said it was Polly,' Clementine said.

Mrs Dent placed the milk and a plump brownie in front of Clementine.

'No, no, there's no Polly,' Mrs Dent said, shaking her head. 'You don't need to worry about that.'

Clementine sighed. 'Phew. When Aunt Violet first brought Pharaoh to our house I thought he was a snake and I was really worried that he might want to eat Lavender for dinner.'

'Pharaoh loves that pig,' said Aunt Violet, looking up from the book she was reading. 'Oh, I wonder how my baby's getting on.'

'I'm sure Mrs Mogg's spoiling him rotten and he's having a wonderful time,' said Lady Clarissa.

'Clementine, was Freddy playing with you too?' asked Mrs Dent. She opened the oven to check on the roast inside.

The child shook her head. 'No. Della said that he was tied up.'

'Oh no, not again!' Mrs Dent slammed the oven door. 'Poor boy. I'll be back in a minute. Digby, can you watch the stove, please?'

In a flash Mrs Dent was gone.

MEMORIES

Mrs Dent returned to the kitchen a short while later with Freddy and Della in tow. The girl's eyes were red-rimmed and her cheeks were puffy.

Mrs Dent headed for the stove to take over from Uncle Digby. Della walked straight to the biscuit barrel and removed the lid.

'No, Della,' her grandmother said without turning her attention from the stove. 'You and your brother can set the table in the dining room, please.'

'I'll help the youngsters,' said Uncle Digby.

The old woman smiled at him. 'Thank you, Digby. I'm a bit behind, I'm afraid.'

'I thought you were on holidays, Uncle Digby,' Clementine said.

'I am. But Mrs Dent has a lot to do and you know I can't sit still for long,' he replied.

'That's true,' Clementine said. 'Uncle Digby's always busy at home. He polishes the silver a lot.'

Lady Clarissa asked if she could help their host with anything else. Mrs Dent insisted she was fine and suggested the ladies make themselves comfortable in the sitting room until dinner was ready. Clementine gathered up Lavender, who had found herself a warm spot beside the oven. She followed her mother and Aunt Violet down the hall and into the front room. Aunt Violet went back to her book and Lady Clarissa flicked through a magazine.

Board games, colouring pencils and sheets of paper were stacked on a bookshelf in the corner. Clementine decided to draw the rock pools and the octopus she and Freddy had found earlier.

A little while later, Freddy appeared at the door and announced that dinner was ready in the dining room.

Clementine skipped towards the boy, holding her picture.

'Do you like it?' she asked.

Freddy nodded. 'That's cool. I love octopuses.'

The children scooted down to the dining room and took their seats. The tension from earlier had evaporated and everyone was enjoying the delicious roast lamb and vegetables.

This time Clementine was sitting between her mother and Freddy, and Della was at the other end of the table next to her grandmother.

'So, children, where do you live?' Uncle Digby asked.

'In Parsley Vale,' Freddy said.

'Our father is the boss of the whole town,' Della said smugly.

Aunt Violet looked up and arched her left eyebrow. 'Oh, really. What does he do?'

'He's hardly that, Della. You must stop exaggerating,' her grandmother tutted.

Della wrinkled her nose.

'He's the Inspector Chief of the police,' said Freddy.

'No, he's not,' Della snapped. He's the Chief Inspector. Anyway, I got to ride in the police car really fast with the siren on.'

'Well, that sounds dangerous,' Uncle Digby said.

Della nodded. 'It was. We were chasing after a bank robber.'

Aunt Violet and Lady Clarissa exchanged frowns.

'You weren't even there,' Freddy said.

'Yes, I was,' Della spat. 'You don't know anything.'

'Della, perhaps you should stop telling stories and eat your dinner,' suggested Mrs Dent.

Della poked her tongue out at Freddy and made a face at Clementine.

There was a squeak and a grunt and Lavender waddled into the room.

'Oh, you really are the most precious creature,' said Mrs Dent as the little pig sniffed her way around the table. 'Do you have any other pets, Clementine?'

The child shook her head. 'Aunt Violet has Pharaoh. He's a sphynx.'

'Why didn't you bring him too?' Mrs Dent asked.

'Pharaoh is something of a Houdini,' said Aunt Violet.

'Oh, an escape artist,' Mrs Dent said, smiling.

Clementine nodded. 'Hopefully he doesn't escape from Mrs Mogg's house.'

'Oh, Clementine, please don't even say such a thing. I don't know what I'd do if anything happened to my darling boy.' Aunt Violet brushed a hand over her eyes.

'It's just a stupid cat,' Della said.

Aunt Violet stared at the girl in horror. 'How dare you? Pharaoh is anything but a stupid cat. He's intelligent and he's sweet and . . .'

'He's ugly but, you know, I've got used to him now. He's really quite lovely,' Clementine added.

Aunt Violet glared at Clementine. Her mother and Uncle Digby tried hard not to smile. If there was one thing they could always rely on, it was Clementine's honesty.

'Goodness,' Mrs Dent laughed. 'You just reminded me of another funny pet, Clementine. When I was a little girl my cousin Teddy had a –'

'Salamander,' Digby Pertwhistle finished the woman's sentence.

Mrs Dent looked surprised. 'That's exactly right.'

'How did you know that, Uncle Digby?' Clementine asked.

The man grinned. 'Rosamund, were you by any chance called Mozzie as a girl?'

A huge smile spread across the woman's face, as if that one word had opened a vault of memories. 'Oh, my goodness. I've got it. You're Diggy,' she said and began to laugh.

Aunt Violet rolled her eyes. 'Diggy and Mozzie, good gracious.'

'But how do you know each other?' Clementine asked.

Mrs Dent took a sip of water and then began the story. 'We were just children. I was about eight or nine.'

'And I would have been twelve,' Uncle Digby added.

'Your Uncle Digby came to stay with my cousin Teddy, here in this house. It was my aunt and uncle's holiday home. They were much better off than we were and my parents were always happy for me to stay with the "posh relatives", as they called them.'

'Teddy and I teased little Mozzie constantly,' Digby Pertwhistle said.

'And I adored the pair of them.' Mrs Dent smiled. 'I was like a puppy following them around everywhere.'

'Has anything changed?' Aunt Violet mumbled to herself.

'Why didn't you see each other again after that?' Clementine asked.

Uncle Digby began to explain. 'Teddy went off to boarding school. I don't know why we lost touch. My parents used to bring me to

Endersley-on-Sea every summer but Teddy was never here.'

'My uncle took a job overseas so the house was hardly ever used, as I recall. Teddy and his sisters spent their holidays in Greece after that. Gosh, I adored Teddy and Diggy. I used to spy on the pair of you when you played cards. Diggy was a very handsome lad.'

Uncle Digby's cheeks flushed. 'Oh, get off with you. My ears stuck out far too much and I was as tall and skinny as a string bean.'

'You could get married,' Clementine said. 'Uncle Digby never had a wife and your husband died, so you could.'

'Clementine, what ridiculous twaddle are you talking about now?' Aunt Violet snapped. 'As if Mrs Dent would want to marry Pertwhistle. He's hardly a catch, is he?'

But Rosamund Dent had a twinkle in her eye. 'I don't know, Miss Appleby. I'd say any woman would be lucky to have him. I'm surprised you haven't snapped him up.'

Aunt Violet shuddered.

'Aunt Violet doesn't need another husband. She's already had three,' Clementine said.

'Clementine! I'll thank you to keep my personal business private,' Aunt Violet huffed.

Digby stood up and began to clear the plates.

'Thank you, *Diggy*. I'll organise dessert,' Mrs Dent said.

'What is it?' Della asked.

'Lemon meringue pie and ice-cream,' said Mrs Dent.

'You said we could have chocolate pudding,' Della whined.

'And I think you could have an early bed time,' Aunt Violet said sternly.

TO THE BEACH

A sliver of sunlight shone through the small gap in the curtains in the front bedroom. Clementine yawned and stretched her arms above her head. She'd dreamt about building a sandcastle and couldn't wait to get to the beach. She was looking forward to testing out the pretty red polka-dot swimming costume Mrs Mogg had made her, too. The kind woman had even sewn a matching hat for Lavender. Aunt Violet had said there was no way she was going to the beach with a pig in a bonnet.

'Hello sleepyhead,' said Lady Clarissa. She put her book on the side table and pushed back the bedcovers.

Clementine rolled over on her own single bed, which was beside her mother's, and blinked her eyes awake. 'Hello Mummy.'

'Did you sleep well, darling?'

Clementine nodded. 'I was tired.'

'Well, you and Freddy did stay up quite late playing cards,' her mother reminded her.

Lady Clarissa and Clementine put on their swimming costumes. Clarissa popped a yellow sundress over the top and Clementine had a matching polka dot dress to put on over her bathers. Clementine picked up Lavender's red lead and the happy trio set off downstairs for breakfast.

'Goodness me, I thought you two were going to sleep the day away,' Aunt Violet said as she set her teacup down with a light thud.

Uncle Digby looked up from his newspaper, pulled a face at Violet and smiled hello to Clarissa and Clementine.

'I suppose that's why it's called a holiday, Aunt Violet,' Clarissa said. 'I haven't slept in for years.'

Clementine thought it was strange for Aunt Violet to talk about sleeping in. At home she did it all the time.

'We're going to the beach,' the child announced. 'Are you coming too?'

'Yes, I think I might,' Aunt Violet replied.

Clementine clapped her hands in delight. 'Will you come swimming?'

'Clementine, I haven't been swimming in the sea since I was a teenager. I'm not about to start again now.'

The child's face dropped.

'Oh, don't look like that. I might wade in the shallows but that's all,' the old woman said.

'I like your dress,' said Clementine, admiring Aunt Violet's aqua-blue kaftan.

'Yes, I haven't had a chance to wear it since the cruise,' Aunt Violet replied. She was referring to her three-month trip aboard the *Queen Mary 2*. Lady Clarissa had won the holiday in a competition and kindly given it to her aunt.

'Where's Mrs Dent?' Clementine asked.

'She's gone to get the children up,' said Uncle Digby.

'Are you coming to the beach too, Uncle Digby?' Clementine asked.

The old man nodded.

'Will *you* take me swimming?' she begged.

'Sweetheart, I'll take you,' her mother said. 'Please stop badgering Aunt Violet and Uncle Digby. Remember, they're on holidays too and they can do whatever they like.'

'You know what, Clementine. I used to love bodysurfing on this beach. I might just dig out my swimming trunks and join you,' Digby said with a grin.

Aunt Violet's face contorted.

'Is something the matter, Aunt Violet?' said Clementine.

'I don't need to see a great tall prune on the beach. Prunes belong at the breakfast table.'

'Who are you calling a prune?' Digby Pertwhistle asked.

'You, you silly old fool,' Aunt Violet scoffed.

'I'll have you know there are quite a few muscles under this shirt.' Uncle Digby raised his left arm and flexed his biceps.

Clementine giggled. 'Uncle Digby, you don't have any muscles –'

'Thank you, Clementine. I thought you'd be sticking up for me.' The old man grinned.

'– but Aunt Violet has more wrinkles than you.' The rest of the sentence was out of her mouth before she had time to stop it.

'I do not,' Aunt Violet retorted. 'Pertwhistle's got wrinkles on his wrinkles.'

The kitchen door flew open and Freddy rushed into the room. He was followed by his sister, who seemed to be dragging her feet. Freddy sat down next to Clementine, but Della stalked to the other end of the table and ignored everyone completely.

Mrs Dent entered next, her face shining. 'Good morning, Clarissa and Clementine.'

Lavender squeaked.

'And you too, Lavender.'

'Hello Mrs Dent,' Clementine and her mother said in unison.

'It's a beautiful day,' the woman declared, 'but I believe we could be in for a storm this afternoon.'

'Are you taking us to the beach too, Granny?' Freddy asked.

'No, darling. I'm sorry, but I have a lot to do this morning.'

'But you always have a lot to do,' the boy moaned.

Clementine looked at him and smiled. 'You can come with us.'

Clementine and Freddy had been talking about exploring the cave before they went to bed last night.

'Yes, of course he can. And Della too,' said Lady Clarissa.

On hearing her name, the girl glanced up at Clementine. Clementine's tummy twinged again, just as it had the day before.

'Oh, Clarissa, are you sure?' Mrs Dent asked.

'Yes, of course. Uncle Digby and Aunt Violet are coming along so there'll be plenty of eyes to keep watch.'

'Would you like to go?' Mrs Dent asked her grandchildren.

The boy nodded furiously.

Della shrugged. 'I suppose so.'

Freddy beamed at Clementine. 'I'll get my bucket and spade,' he said, then leaned over and whispered to Clementine, 'and my torch.'

'We can make a sandcastle,' Clementine said. 'I'll take my bucket and spade too.'

Breakfast was over quickly. Mrs Dent insisted on packing some freshly baked chocolate cake and honey jumbles, along with the leftover brownies and some apples and bananas. She added a thermos of tea and some cold drinks too.

Uncle Digby retrieved the cooler bag, umbrella and jazzy blue beach chairs that had been Lady Clarissa's most recent competition win.

Della and Freddy reappeared with their swimmers on underneath their clothes. Freddy's face was lathered white with sunscreen.

Mrs Dent took her grandchildren to one side. 'Now, you make sure that you do everything you're asked, please. I don't want to hear any reports of bad behaviour. And have you put on sunscreen, Della?'

'Yes,' the child grouched. 'I don't get sunburnt, anyway.'

Mrs Dent gave her granddaughter a sceptical look, then turned to Lady Clarissa.

'Thank you, Clarissa. I do appreciate having some time to catch up on the paperwork,' the old woman said.

'It's a pleasure. Believe me, I know how hard it is to get all the jobs done when you have a house full of guests,' Lady Clarissa replied.

Aunt Violet had disappeared upstairs and returned wearing the most enormous blue sunhat.

'Good heavens,' Uncle Digby gasped. 'Do

you realise there's a flying saucer on your head, Miss Appleby?'

Clementine laughed out loud.

'You know absolutely nothing about fashion, do you, Pertwhistle?' The old woman rolled her eyes behind her dark glasses.

'Uncle Digby, I think Aunt Violet looks beautiful,' Clementine said admiringly.

'As long as she doesn't injure anyone on the street, I suppose,' Uncle Digby teased. 'She could take someone's head off with that thing.'

'And what are you wearing?' Aunt Violet looked the old man up and down. 'I doubt those twig legs of yours have seen the sun since you were a boy.'

Clementine had never seen Uncle Digby in shorts before either. His legs *were* a bit like a seagull's, she decided.

'That's it. I'm calling a truce. It's about time you two tried to be nice to one another,' Lady Clarissa said sternly.

Uncle Digby hung his head. 'Oh, all right. I'll do my best.'

'If I must,' Aunt Violet agreed.

Clementine and her mother looked at each other and smiled.

'I think we should be off,' said Lady Clarissa. She bustled about taking charge of her motley crew.

Clementine and Freddy walked ahead with Lavender, and Aunt Violet and Uncle Digby came behind.

'So tell me, Della, are you having a lovely holiday?' Lady Clarissa asked as she closed the garden gate behind her. 'It must be nice to spend time with your granny.'

'Not really,' the child replied. 'Granny's bossy and boring.'

'Oh,' Clarissa mouthed. It seemed that Della might be a little harder to thaw than she'd thought.

NEW FRIENDS

The beach was dotted with families staking out their spots, but there was still lots of space. Aunt Violet led the way down the sand. She found a patch far enough from the water that she wouldn't have to worry about any splashes.

Uncle Digby pitched the new blue beach umbrella while the others rolled out their towels and unfolded the three low beach chairs. Aunt Violet lowered herself onto her chair and immediately pulled a fashion magazine from her oversized beach bag.

Della plonked herself onto the sand beside her brother and proceeded to lecture him. 'We're going to build a mermaid's castle and I'm going to be the mermaid princess.'

'But I don't want to do that,' Freddy said. 'I don't even know what a mermaid's castle looks like.'

Freddy and Clementine were eager to go back to the rock pools and have a proper look in the cave, but Freddy didn't want Della to come. She would just take over, as always.

'We should do what she says and then we can go and look at the cave later,' Clementine whispered to Freddy.

The boy nodded. 'We want to build a proper castle,' he told his sister.

'No, it's a mermaid's castle. I'm in charge because I'm the oldest,' the girl insisted. 'I'll tell you what to do.'

Lady Clarissa cleared her throat. 'Darling, have you put sunscreen on Lavender yet?' The sun already had a bite to it.

Clementine nodded. Lavender was sitting on the towel beside her.

'Sunscreen? On a pig?' Della scoffed.

'Lavender gets sunburnt more easily than you and me,' Clementine explained. 'That's why pigs roll in mud – to protect their skin. Lavender doesn't like mud very much, so we have to put sunscreen on her.'

'That's stupid,' Della said. 'Pigs aren't proper pets, anyway.'

Freddy ignored his sister and grinned at Clementine. 'Does Lavender have a sunhat?'

She nodded and rushed over to pull it from her mother's beach bag.

'That's ridiculous,' Della snorted as Clementine put the little bonnet on Lavender's head.

'I think she looks cute,' Freddy said.

Della ignored her brother and stood up. 'Come on then, you'd better get the buckets and spades and start building my mermaid's castle.'

Clementine and Freddy did as they were told.

'We're building it right there.' Della pointed at a spot a little closer to the water. 'Now, this is what it has to look like. I want a proper castle with towers and turrets and then there has to be a mermaid's tail next to it and when it's finished I'll be the body and you have to dig underneath so my legs are covered by the tail . . .'

The girl's voice droned on and on. Freddy thought it sounded very complicated.

'Mummy, can you look after Lavender?' Clementine asked.

'Of course, darling.' Lady Clarissa took the little pig's lead and lashed it to her beach chair.

Lavender squealed as Clementine rushed off to catch up with Freddy.

'When you want to go for a swim, come and let me know,' Lady Clarissa called after Clementine. 'And don't wander off.'

Della stood with her hands on her hips and ordered Freddy to start digging. She directed Clementine to fill the buckets with water so they could shape the sand. Clemmie ran to the surf's edge and back several times while Della stood like a policeman directing traffic.

As the mermaid's tail took shape, Clementine's and Freddy's faces grew red and beads of sweat trickled down their temples.

'It doesn't look right,' Della whined. 'You need to make a scaly pattern.'

'Maybe you could find some shells to decorate the tail?' Clementine suggested.

'I *already* thought of that,' Della said, rolling her eyes. But she raced down the beach all the same.

'Your sister's bossy,' Clementine said.

Freddy nodded. 'She'd be even worse if you weren't here.'

Clementine wondered how much more horrible the girl could be. She felt very sorry for Freddy.

The two children were busy working on their construction and didn't see a group of girls approaching.

'That looks amazing,' gasped one girl. She

had cascading chocolate curls and brown eyes as big as saucers.

Clementine looked up and shielded her eyes from the sun. 'Thank you,' she said.

'Do you want some help?' asked another girl. She had red hair and freckles, and wore a white sunhat.

Freddy nodded. 'Yes, please.'

'My name's Alice-Miranda Highton-Smith-Kennington-Jones,' the brown-haired girl said. 'This is Millie.' She pointed at the red-haired girl. 'And that's Jacinta.' She pointed at a taller blonde-haired girl.

Millie and Jacinta both said hello.

'What are your names?' Jacinta asked.

'I'm Clementine Rose.'

'And I'm Freddy,' the boy answered.

'Are you brother and sister?' Alice-Miranda asked.

Freddy smiled.

Clementine did too. 'No, we just met yester-day,' she said.

'You look like twins,' said Jacinta.

'We're having a holiday in Millie's caravan, just up there,' Alice-Miranda said.

'I'd like to stay in a caravan but I don't think Aunt Violet would like it,' said Clementine.

'Who's Aunt Violet?' Millie asked.

'She's my grandpa's sister and she's very old and Mummy once said that she was crusty like a barnacle,' Clementine explained.

The three girls giggled, imagining an old lady covered in little shells.

'Do you want to help build the tower?' Freddy asked.

Alice-Miranda nodded. The girls pitched in and soon they had a very impressive castle next to the mermaid's tail.

'Do you live far away?' Alice-Miranda asked the children.

'In Parsley Vale,' Freddy said.

Clementine nodded. 'I live in Penberthy Floss.'

'Really?' said Alice-Miranda. 'That's just next to the village I live in, Highton Mill. And Parsley Vale is close to our boarding school too.'

'I go to Ellery Prep,' Clementine said.

'What a lovely coincidence. I went there too and my friend Poppy goes there now. She and her brother and mummy and daddy live on our farm,' Alice-Miranda explained.

'Really?' Clementine said excitedly. 'Poppy's my friend too!'

'You'll have to come and visit her in the holidays. I could take you riding on my pony, Bonaparte,' Alice-Miranda offered.

Clementine nodded. She'd never been on a horse before but she was keen to try.

Lady Clarissa untied Lavender's lead and walked the little pig towards the group of children. 'Hello,' she said, smiling at the girls and Freddy. 'I see you're making friends.'

Alice-Miranda introduced herself and the other girls to Lady Clarissa.

'Is that a teacup pig?' Millie's eyes were almost popping out of her head.

'Yes. Her name's Lavender,' Clementine said.

'She's adorable.' Millie scooped the little pig into her arms.

Lady Clarissa looked around and realised that Della was missing. 'Where's your sister, Freddy?'

He shrugged. Lady Clarissa scanned the beach.

'Della went to find some shells,' said Clementine.

Clarissa's heart pounded. She'd promised to keep a close eye on the children for Mrs Dent.

'Who's Della?' Alice-Miranda asked.

'She's my sister,' Freddy said.

'We can help you look for her,' said Alice-Miranda. 'Don't worry, I'm sure she can't have gone far.'

Lady Clarissa's eyes searched the crowd. She wasn't nearly as sure as Alice-Miranda.

BEASTLY CREATURES

Just as the group was about to set off, a piercing scream sliced the air. The beach-goers looked towards the noise and several people leapt to their feet.

A young lifeguard sprinted towards the water.

'Help!' a voice shouted.

'Oh no, that's Della!' Lady Clarissa spun around and raced towards the growing crowd of onlookers.

She pushed her way through the people, with Clementine and Freddy close behind her.

Alice-Miranda and Jacinta followed. Millie stayed back, holding onto Lavender.

'Della, what happened? Are you hurt?' Lady Clarissa looked at the child, whose face was the colour of a tomato.

The lifeguard was doing his best to calm the girl. 'Miss, did something sting you?' A swarm of jellyfish had been sighted further up the coast.

'It was in the water,' the child sobbed. 'It wrapped around my leg.'

The tall man directed the crowd of onlookers to stand back as he scanned the shallows. 'Was it a stinger or a jellyfish?' he asked. He couldn't see any marks on the girl.

'I don't know!' Della cried. She turned around to look at the surf. 'It could have been a shark. There it is!' She pointed.

'Seaweed?' the lifeguard asked, a bewildered look on his face. 'Is that all?'

'What do you mean?' Della yelled. 'It was beastly. It wrapped around my leg and pulled me out into the water and it made me drop all my shells and now I haven't got any for the mermaid's tail.'

Clementine noticed a pile of shells being tossed about as the water came in and was sucked back out again.

The young man frowned at Della and then turned to the crowd. 'All right, folks, everything's fine. There's nothing to see here.'

Freddy sighed. He turned and walked back up the sand.

'Della, why don't you come and have a drink and something to eat?' Lady Clarissa said kindly. She noticed the child's bright pink shoulders and face. 'Did you put any sunscreen on this morning?'

'Yes, of course I did. It just didn't work,' Della sniffed.

Clementine raced back to their mermaid castle and grabbed a bucket. She ran to the water's edge and tried to gather up as many of the shells as she could see.

Lady Clarissa guided Della up the beach. 'Come on, I think I'll take you home. That sunburn looks nasty.'

Tears were streaming down the child's face. 'My leg hurts,' Della sniffled. She wiped her nose with the back of her hand and reached down to scratch her thigh. 'Something did sting me. It wasn't just the seaweed.'

Lady Clarissa stopped and inspected Della's leg. 'I'm sure your grandmother will have some calamine lotion.'

Lady Clarissa turned and called back to Clementine, 'Clemmie, why don't you take your friends up to our umbrella. Tell Aunt Violet and Uncle Digby that I'm taking Della home and ask them to keep an eye on you and Freddy. You can all have some drinks and a snack.'

The child nodded. Her mother and Della walked away up the beach.

Clementine led her new friends to where Aunt Violet and Uncle Digby were sitting.

'Hello Aunt Violet,' Clementine shouted as she bounded up to her chair.

The woman gave a snort. 'Good heavens, Clementine, you don't need to scare me half to death.'

'Were you asleep?'

'Of course not.' Aunt Violet sat up straighter.

'Mummy said that we could have something to eat and a drink.' She motioned towards her friends.

'Are we taking in orphans?' Aunt Violet asked. She tapped her foot on Uncle Digby's bare leg. The man was snoring gently.

He grunted awake. 'Yes, yes, what is it?'

'We've got to feed the children. I don't know where Clarissa has swanned off to,' Aunt Violet grumbled.

'Mummy's taken Della home because she's got a sunburn,' Clementine said. 'And she asked if you could look after us.'

Aunt Violet grimaced. Uncle Digby dug around inside the cooler bag and handed drinks to the children.

'Hello, I'm Alice-Miranda Highton-Smith-Kennington-Jones,' one of the new girls said. She offered her hand to Aunt Violet.

The woman perked up immediately. 'Did you say Highton-Smith-Kennington-Jones?'

Alice-Miranda nodded.

'Oh, how lovely to meet you.' Aunt Violet took the child's tiny hand into hers and gave it a shake. 'We're practically neighbours, you know. We're at Penberthy House.'

Alice-Miranda smiled and introduced her friends.

Jacinta stepped forward to say hello and tripped on the edge of a towel. She went flying and sent sand all over Aunt Violet.

The woman's face contorted.

'I'm sorry,' Jacinta said meekly.

'So you should be,' Aunt Violet tutted.

The children enjoyed their snacks and then went back to the sandcastle. They decorated it happily until Millie's mother called the older girls to go in.

'We're leaving tomorrow morning,' Alice-Miranda explained. 'But I'm sure I'll see you again at home, Clementine.'

Clementine hoped so too. She and Freddy farewelled their new friends.

'Do you want to go and look at the cave now?' Freddy asked Clementine.

The girl nodded. 'But we'll have to take Uncle Digby or Aunt Violet.'

'Yes, but they can just have a rest where your mother did yesterday,' said Freddy. He didn't want the grown-ups spoiling their adventure.

Clementine returned a minute later with Uncle Digby in tow. 'You don't have to come all the way with us, Uncle Digby. There's a big rock you can sit on.'

'All right, then. Can I bring my book?' the old man asked.

Clementine nodded.

Uncle Digby walked back to their camp site to get it.

'Where's Lavender?' Freddy asked.

'She's asleep. Aunt Violet said that she'd look after her.'

Clementine and Freddy were armed with buckets in case they found any treasure to bring back, and Freddy had the little torch in the pocket of his board shorts.

Uncle Digby walked back to the children.

'Don't worry, Uncle Digby, we'll be very careful,' Clementine told the old man. She grabbed hold of Freddy's hand and they ran off towards the rocks.

A THRILLING DISCOVERY

Freddy and Clementine hopped over the rocks just as they had done the day before. The pools of water sparkled in the sun as Clementine crouched down to look for the octopus. It was doing a good job of hiding. She could only see some shells and a couple of tiny crabs.

'Come on, Clementine,' Freddy shouted as he jumped from rock to rock.

She caught up to him where the rock shelf curved around the small headland.

To get to the cave, they had to climb down to a lower level. Clementine noticed that the waves were bigger now and every few minutes the surf would spray upwards, sending a shower of sea water onto the edge of the platform. A little channel ran between the rocks and cave's mouth, but there was only a trickle of water in it.

Clementine and Freddy hopped down onto the sand.

'Do you really think there could be treasure inside?' Clementine asked, her eyes wide.

Freddy shrugged. 'I didn't find any last time, but I didn't have a torch then so I couldn't see properly. Granny says there used to be pirates on this coast a long time ago.'

Clementine's tummy fluttered. This really was a proper adventure.

Freddy took the torch out of his pocket. He pulled the vines back from the cave entrance and shone the light inside. Then he took Clementine's hand and the two children crept inside.

'It smells awful,' Clementine whispered.

Freddy held his nose. 'Yuck! Like dead fish.'

He shone the light straight ahead of them. Five rectangular stones stuck out of the sand like giant's teeth. Then he directed the torch at the sandy floor and up to the smooth curve of the roof. It didn't look like there was any treasure. Just a couple of empty soft-drink bottles lying in the sand. The cave wasn't nearly as deep as Freddy had hoped, either.

Clementine squeezed Freddy's hand. 'It's really smelly in here. Do you want to go back for a swim?'

He nodded.

Just as the children turned to leave, Freddy's torchlight caught something unexpected.

'Did you see that?' he asked.

'What?' Clementine whispered.

Freddy pointed the torch back to the same spot. Poking out from behind one of the stones were two red eyes. They glowed in the darkness.

'What's that?' the boy breathed.

'I don't know.' Clementine's heart was pounding.

All of a sudden there was a strange barking sound.

Freddy squinted. 'It must be a puppy.'

'What if it's lost?' Clementine said. 'We should help it.'

'Maybe I can keep it?' Freddy felt a rush of excitement as he imagined a new pet. He loved Lavender and had been planning to ask his parents if he could have a pet pig – but a dog might be even better.

'Here, boy,' Freddy said soothingly.

The two children walked closer to the creature. It had a long body and a funny oval head with tiny little ears sticking out at the sides.

'That's a strange-looking dog,' Clementine said.

The creature barked again and stretched upwards. It danced from one side to the other.

'That's not a dog,' Freddy gasped. 'It's a seal.'

Clementine didn't know much about seals, but this one was small and very cute. She walked closer and reached out.

'No!' Freddy said. 'He's a wild animal. You can't touch him.'

Clementine jumped back.

'We learned about seals at school,' Freddy said. 'If people pet them, they get confused.'

'What do they eat?' Clementine asked.

'Fish,' Freddy replied.

'Oh! That's why it's so stinky in here,' Clementine said. 'Do you think it's lost?'

'I don't know,' Freddy said with a shrug. 'There are lots of seals on the next beach around from here. He looks okay. Maybe he's just having some time out from a bossy sister.'

Clementine giggled. 'Do you think we should tell Uncle Digby?'

Freddy watched as the creature swayed from side to side.

'You know, he could be our special secret,' Freddy said. He liked the idea of having something only he and Clementine knew about.

Clementine nodded. 'Okay.'

The seal looked at the children with its big brown eyes.

'Come on, Freddy, we should go or Uncle Digby might get worried.' Clementine tugged at the boy's arm.

The two children left the cave and scrambled back up onto the higher rock ledge. They trod carefully between the pools.

Freddy's eyes were still shining with excitement. 'That was so cool!'

'I know,' Clementine said.

'Hello there,' said Uncle Digby as the children approached. 'I was just about to come and find you. I thought you might like to go for a swim and then we can get some lunch.'

'You should have seen what we found, Uncle Digby,' Clementine burst out.

Freddy nudged her and frowned.

'What was it?' the old man asked.

'I can't tell you because it's a secret,' she said.

'Oh, I see,' Uncle Digby said seriously as he tried not to smile.

FISH AND CHIPS

'I can't remember the last time I had fish and chips on the beach,' Aunt Violet said as she waved a plump chip in the air.

Uncle Digby had taken Clementine and Freddy to Mr Alessi's to buy fish and chips for their lunch. In the meantime, Lady Clarissa had returned to the beach. She had left Della at home with her grandmother, whining about her sore leg and sunburn.

Clementine watched a seagull that had landed close by. It was stalking around their camp.

Her great-aunt popped her chip into her mouth and reached for another. This time she wasn't quick enough. The cheeky grey-and-white gull raced in and plucked the tasty morsel from her fingertips.

'Good heavens!' Aunt Violet turned to face the feathered thief. 'Get away from me, you horrid beast.'

Everyone laughed. Lavender ran towards the bird, grunting and squealing.

Uncle Digby grinned. 'Perhaps you shouldn't wave your chips around like a conductor's baton, Miss Appleby.'

Aunt Violet leaned forward to protect her food. 'Thank you, Lavender – at least you're looking after me.' She offered the little pig a chip.

Fortunately, one of the Alessi Brothers' fishing boats puttered into the harbour a minute later. Every seagull on the beach flew over to see if any undersized treats would be thrown to them.

Just as the group finished their lunch, dark clouds rolled across the sky and thunder

rumbled out at sea. Lady Clarissa gathered up the towels. Even Aunt Violet pitched in by folding the chairs. Uncle Digby just managed to grab hold of the beach umbrella as the wind whipped it out of the sand.

'We'd best make a run for it,' Lady Clarissa called.

The group scrambled along the beach, up the steps and across the road. Lavender squealed and wriggled in Clementine's arms. Freddy ran down the garden path and pushed open the front door just as the rain began to belt down.

'Well, that was good timing,' Lady Clarissa puffed. She directed the children to rub the sand off their feet and legs before they entered the hall.

'Oh, there you are!' Mrs Dent rushed towards them. 'I was beginning to worry. Come and I'll get you some tea.'

'Is there somewhere I can put all this?' Uncle Digby was balancing the umbrella, the beach chairs and a pile of towels.

'There's a utility room at the end of the hall.'

Mrs Dent had the kettle on in no time and poured two glasses of orange juice for Clementine and Freddy.

'How's Della?' Lady Clarissa asked.

'The child has managed to get herself burnt to a crisp. Clearly she did not have sunscreen on this morning when I asked her. Now she's going to pay for it. In fact, I think she might have a touch of sunstroke,' Mrs Dent tutted.

'What about her leg?' Lady Clarissa asked.

Mrs Dent frowned. 'I think that was just some completely harmless seaweed. It might be a bit scratchy, but that's all. Anyway, how was the rest of your day?'

'It was great!' Clementine exclaimed. 'We made some new friends and we went exploring and we found –'

'Crabs!' Freddy said, giving Clementine a secret look.

'Well, it sounds like you've had a very adventurous day, my dears,' Mrs Dent said as she hopped up to refill the teapot.

'And another five to go,' Clementine said.

Freddy's face fell. 'Only five?'

'We have to go home on Sunday,' said Clementine.

Freddy didn't ever want Clementine to go home. He wondered if Lady Clarissa would consider taking Della instead.

ESCAPE

The rain lashed the coast for hours. Freddy and Clementine played Old Maid in the kitchen. Mrs Dent cooked dinner while she and Uncle Digby chatted about their childhoods. Aunt Violet and Lady Clarissa read in the sitting room. Della stayed in her room. She didn't come down for dinner either. Mrs Dent took her a tray. She returned saying that the child was utterly miserable with her sunburn.

'Will the storm be gone by tomorrow?' Clementine asked Mrs Dent.

'It should be. Storms like this usually come in a fury and leave just as quickly.'

But Mrs Dent was wrong. The next morning, Clementine looked out her bedroom window and discovered a grey, dreary day.

'No beach today,' she sighed and turned to her mother, who was lying in bed.

'No, darling. But there are plenty of things you can do inside.'

Freddy and Clementine spent the morning playing board games in the sitting room with Uncle Digby and Lady Clarissa. Even Aunt Violet joined in for a round of Snakes and Ladders. Della stayed upstairs, ringing a bell constantly for her grandmother, until Mrs Dent stumped upstairs for the fifth time and brought the bell back down with her.

After lunch, Freddy and Clementine decided to do some drawing at the kitchen table. Clementine started drawing a picture of a seal, with great big brown eyes and little flippers.

'I think the ears are cute,' she said to Freddy. He was drawing an octopus strangling a crab.

'What do you think, Lavender?' Clementine held up her picture. The little pig looked up and grunted.

The kitchen door flew open and Della stalked into the room. 'Where's Granny?'

'I don't know,' Freddy said with a shrug.

'I want something to eat.' Della yanked open the refrigerator door and peered inside.

A huge fish stared up at her from a platter.

'Pooh! I hate fish.'

She slammed the door and went to the biscuit tin, where she found two chocolate brownies.

'Are you feeling better?' Clementine asked. The girl's face was bright red.

'Sort of,' Della said. She walked back to the table and stood beside Clementine, looking at the child's drawing.

'It's a seal,' Clementine said.

'I know that,' Della replied. She wasn't about to say so, but she thought it was a good picture for a five-year-old.

'I saw a seal at the beach,' Della bragged, before taking a big bite of brownie.

'When?' asked Freddy.

'You weren't there,' Della said.

'I don't believe you,' Freddy retorted. 'You've never seen a seal. But we have.' He clamped his hands over his mouth but it was too late. The words had already escaped.

Clementine looked at Freddy.

'When?' Della asked, narrowing her eyes.

Freddy ignored her and kept drawing.

'Now who's telling lies?' Della said smartly.

Clementine couldn't stay quiet any longer. 'He's not lying. We saw a seal in a cave yesterday, after you went home.'

'Really? Show me,' Della demanded.

'It probably won't be there any more,' Clementine said. 'But it was so sweet.'

'I want to see the seal,' Della said, stamping her foot.

Clementine looked out the kitchen window at the steely sky. 'It's raining.'

Della rolled her eyes. 'We've got raincoats. Come on.'

'I don't think Mummy will let me go out,' said Clementine. 'She's upstairs having a rest.'

'You're such a baby,' Della scoffed.

'She is not,' Freddy said, his eyebrows knitting together fiercely.

'You're both babies,' Della spat. 'I'm going to see this seal whether you come or not.'

'You won't even find it,' Freddy said, as his sister stormed out of the kitchen.

Clementine stared at Freddy. 'Are you going to tell your granny?'

Freddy shook his head. 'I don't care if she goes. She won't see anything. She didn't even take a torch.'

Both children went back to drawing. A few minutes later, Clementine glanced around the room. 'Where's Lavender?'

Freddy peered around the room too. 'I don't know. She was here before.'

Clementine slipped down from her chair and walked around the kitchen, searching beside the stove and under the table.

'She's not here,' Clementine said, frowning. She went into the hallway and glanced towards the front door. 'Freddy! Come quick!'

Freddy flew out of his seat and into the hall. The front door was wide open.

'Della!' he called and raced onto the porch.

The front gate was open too.

Clementine stared at the boy, her blue eyes wide. 'Come on. We've got to find Lavender.'

'Wait a minute.' Freddy ran back to the kitchen and grabbed his torch off the bench.

STUCK

The sky was still dark but it had stopped raining. Clementine and Freddy ran out the front gate and across the road to the beach. Clementine's voice rang out. 'Lavender? Lavender!'

Freddy echoed the call.

'She probably followed Della,' he said eventually. 'Don't worry. She can't have gone too far yet.'

Clementine nodded. She hoped he was right.

Freddy looked down to the little beach but it was bare. He and Clementine ran along the wet sand towards the rocks.

'Be careful, Clementine, it's slippery,' the boy warned as they scrambled over the platform.

'Della, where are you?' Freddy called.

'Lavender!' Clementine shouted. She turned around and was relieved to see a little grey figure dashing towards them. Clementine scooped the pig into her arms and kissed the top of her head.

'Thank goodness,' Freddy sighed.

'What about Della?' Clementine asked. 'Do you think she's in the cave?'

'I don't know, but we could have a look.'

The two children picked their way around the headland, then leapt down across the little channel of water onto the tiny beach. Clementine gasped as she almost slipped in. She clutched Lavender tightly and looked back at the rising water. Freddy pulled the creeper back and shone the torchlight inside.

'Della!' he called. His voice echoed. *Della-ella-ella.*

The empty soft-drink bottles were still there but there was no sign of Della or the seal.

'She's not here,' Freddy said. 'We should go back before Granny gets worried.'

Clementine turned around. The sun was peeking through the clouds. The rocks looked shiny and clean and the grass that grew along the edge of the cliff was bright green.

'Freddy, look at the water. It's too high,' Clementine gulped. 'How can we get back?'

Freddy spun around. The little channel separating the curve of beach and the rock platform was filling fast. Water was starting to force its way into the cave as well.

'The tide's coming in,' he said.

'What does that mean?' asked Clementine. She was holding Lavender tight.

'The tide is the sea coming in and going out. The water gets deeper and shallower. But I think we can still get across now.'

Clementine shook her head. 'I'm scared. It's too deep. Is there another way?'

'No, that cliff's too steep. We can't get up there. But it's okay. The water never covers the whole beach. We can wait over there.' Freddy pointed to a grassy spot that met the sand at the end of the tiny beach. 'We're safe. I promise. But we won't be able to get across until the water goes down again.'

Clementine's eyes filled with tears. 'How long does that take?'

Freddy bit his lip. 'I don't know exactly.'

'But Mummy will be worried.' Fat tears began to flow down Clementine's cheeks. Lavender turned and licked the salty drops away.

'Don't worry, Clementine. Someone will come,' the boy said. But Freddy had a terrible feeling that it would be night-time before the tide went out again.

RESCUE

Freddy and Clementine climbed up onto the grassy knoll. Lavender was snorting and looking at the sea. Clementine's stomach was churning.

'Look, there's Della!' Freddy said.

His sister appeared on the top of the rock platform.

Della had thought Freddy would follow her when she stormed out to look for the seal. She hadn't wanted to go to that stinky cave on her own. It was much too dark and scary. But when the boy hadn't appeared she went for a walk around the village. Mrs Lee had given her an ice-cream, which she'd eaten while sitting on the seawall. Then she came to the beach to look for crabs in the rock pools.

'Della!' Freddy called above the sound of the waves.

She looked up and was surprised to see her brother and Clementine on the other side of the channel. 'What are you doing over there?' she called back.

'We're stuck,' the boy shouted.

Della's stomach tightened. Freddy might be a pain sometimes but she didn't want him to be stuck at high tide.

'Don't worry. I'll get help!' the girl shouted. She scurried back across the rocks to the beach.

Lady Clarissa had searched high and low for the children. She was about to go down and check the kitchen once more, when she met Uncle Digby.

'Hello dear,' he greeted her.

'You haven't seen Clementine, have you?'

The old man shook his head. 'Afraid I've been in the land of nod for the past couple of hours.'

Aunt Violet's bedroom door opened and the woman marched outside.

'Is this a party?' she asked her niece and Uncle Digby.

'I'm trying to find the children,' said Lady Clarissa.

'Don't worry. They're probably playing hide-and-seek or some such nonsense.'

Lady Clarissa didn't look convinced. 'It's far too quiet for my liking.'

The three adults walked down to the kitchen.

'Did you find them, dear?' Mrs Dent asked. Lady Clarissa shook her head.

The front door banged.

Mrs Dent breathed a sigh of relief. 'There

you go. They must have been in the garden.'

'Granny, Granny!' Della's voice rang through the house. The child raced into the kitchen.

'What's the matter?' Mrs Dent asked.

'Freddy and Clementine went to find the seal and now they're stuck,' the child blurted.

Aunt Violet pursed her lips. 'What seal?'

'Della, what nonsense are you talking about this time? Have you done something to your brother again?' Mrs Dent frowned.

Della shook her head. 'I promise, Granny, it's true. I'm not making it up.'

Uncle Digby nodded. 'The children did tell me they'd found a cave yesterday.'

'And now the tide's coming in and they're stuck on the tiny beach,' insisted Della.

Lady Clarissa caught her breath. 'What do you mean they're stuck?'

'The water's coming into the channel and Clementine is too small to jump the rocks and she's got Lavender too,' Della blurted.

'Oh, goodness. Come on, Della. Show me,' said Lady Clarissa hurriedly.

'What about some rope?' Aunt Violet suggested. 'Just in case.'

Lady Clarissa stopped. 'That's a great idea, Aunt Violet.'

Mrs Dent rushed off down the hallway to the utility room, and returned with a tightly wound length of rope. She threw the bundle to Clarissa.

'Okay, let's go,' Lady Clarissa said.

Della took off, with Lady Clarissa, Aunt Violet, Uncle Digby and Mrs Dent in pursuit.

Lady Clarissa shouted over her shoulder, 'Uncle Digby, please don't rush.'

'Yes, don't overdo it, Pertwhistle,' said Aunt Violet. 'We don't need you having another trip to the hospital.'

A few minutes later, Lady Clarissa and Della reached the rock shelf. The surf was much bigger than the day before and every couple of minutes a shower sprayed over the ledge.

'Mummy!' Clementine shouted.

'Oh, darling, I'm here,' Lady Clarissa called back. She looked at the little channel, which was getting deeper by the second.

Uncle Digby and the others arrived just as Lady Clarissa was tying the rope securely around her middle.

'Take this.' She handed the end to Uncle Digby.

'Oh, do be careful, Clarissa,' said Aunt Violet, her voice fluttering.

'I think we should all hold on,' Uncle Digby said.

Mrs Dent wrapped her hands around Uncle Digby's waist and Aunt Violet did the same to Mrs Dent. The three of them formed an anchor.

Lady Clarissa stepped down onto the rocks. Water swirled around her feet and she waded into the rushing tide.

'Come as close as you can, sweetheart, and I'll take Lavender first,' Lady Clarissa directed.

Clementine did as she was told and within a minute Lavender was safely on the other side in Della's arms.

'Come on, darling, you're next,' Clarissa urged Clementine towards her. 'Stay there, Freddy. I'll be back for you in a minute.'

'I'm okay,' Freddy called.

Clementine turned and looked at her friend.

'Go on,' he said. 'You'll be all right.'

Clementine reached out towards her mother. Lady Clarissa grabbed Clementine's hand and hauled her across the swirling water. She hugged the child tight.

'I'm sorry, Mummy, I'm sorry,' Clementine sobbed.

Clarissa passed her to Uncle Digby before wading in for the third time. She reached out and grabbed Freddy's hands. Together they scrambled up the rocks to safety.

'Goodness me, whatever were you thinking coming out here on your own?' Aunt Violet admonished the pair.

'I'm just glad you're safe,' Mrs Dent said, giving Freddy a hug.

'We would have been okay,' said Freddy. 'It might have been a bit scary in the dark, that's all.'

'Well, you're lucky Della found you,' Mrs Dent said. 'If that's what really happened.'

Della looked sheepish.

'Della?' Mrs Dent's tone was not to be messed with.

'It's my fault,' Della said, a tear rolling down her cheek.

Freddy and Clementine looked at each other in surprise.

'I said that Freddy and Clementine were babies because they wouldn't take me to see the seal and so I went on my own. But I was too scared. I went to the village instead and then I came to look at the rock pools,' Della said, sniffling.

Lady Clarissa looked at Freddy and Clementine. 'But why did you come here, if you'd already told Della you wouldn't?'

'Because Lavender escaped and we thought she'd followed Della to the cave,' Clementine explained.

Mrs Dent looked at her granddaughter, a swell of disappointment rising in her chest. 'Did you let Lavender out on purpose?'

'No, Granny. I promise I didn't. I thought

I pulled the door shut. But I remember I left the gate open,' Della sniffed. 'I'm sorry. I really am. I love Freddy. He's my brother.'

Aunt Violet looked at Freddy and winked. 'Well, young man, I bet that's not something you hear every day.'

Freddy grinned.

'Did you really find a seal yesterday?' Uncle Digby asked, breaking the tension.

Clementine nodded. She brushed the tears from her eyes and glanced back towards the cave.

As the group had been talking, the tide had risen much higher. Water was now rushing in and out of the little cave.

'Look,' Clementine cried out. 'There it is!'

'You really *did* find a seal!' Della said, her face crumpling into a smile.

The group was amazed to see a little seal bobbing up and down right in front of them. He swam into the cave and shot back out again as fast as a bullet. Then he rolled over and raised his flipper in the air.

Clementine grinned. 'Did that seal just wave at us?'

'I think he did, Clemmie,' Uncle Digby nodded. 'I think he did.'

CAST OF CHARACTERS

The Appleby household

Clementine Rose Appleby	Five-year-old daughter of Lady Clarissa
Lavender	Clemmie's teacup pig
Lady Clarissa Appleby	Clementine's mother and the owner of Penberthy House
Digby Pertwhistle	Butler at Penberthy House
Aunt Violet Appleby	Clementine's grandfather's sister
Pharaoh	Aunt Violet's beloved sphynx cat

Others

Mrs Rosamund Dent	Owner of the Endersley-on-Sea guesthouse
Della Dent	Mrs Dent's granddaughter
Freddy Dent	Mrs Dent's grandson
Lenny Phipps	Tow-truck driver
Alice-Miranda Highton-Smith Kennington-Jones	A new friend
Millie	A new friend
Jacinta	A new friend

ABOUT THE AUTHOR

Jacqueline Harvey taught for many years in girls' boarding schools. She is the author of the bestselling Alice-Miranda series and the Clementine Rose series, and was awarded Honour Book in the 2006 Australian CBC Awards for her picture book *The Sound of the Sea*. She now writes full-time and is working on more Alice-Miranda and Clementine Rose adventures.

www.jacquelineharvey.com.au

Have you read these other stories
about Clementine Rose?

CLEMENTINE ROSE
and the
Surprise Visitor

Jacqueline Harvey

Can Clementine solve the mystery of an unexpected guest?

CLEMENTINE ROSE
and the
Pet Day Disaster

Jacqueline Harvey

Clementine can't wait for her school's special Pet Day.
Will she win a prize?

CLEMENTINE ROSE
and the
Perfect Present

Jacqueline Harvey

Can Clementine fix everything with the perfect present?

CLEMENTINE ROSE
and the
Farm Fiasco

Jacqueline Harvey

Can Clementine save her class trip from disaster?

CLEMENTINE ROSE
and the
Treasure Box

Jacqueline
Harvey

Can Clementine find the hidden treasure?

CLEMENTINE ROSE
and the
Famous Friend

Jacqueline
Harvey

Can Clementine uncover the secret of a mystery visitor?

CLEMENTINE ROSE
and the
Ballet Break-In

Jacqueline
Harvey

Can Clementine help the show go on?